She Sold Her Husband

© 2023 Farlag Press
All rights reserved.

ISBN 9791096677139

English translation © Zeke Levine 2023

"The First Trip to Coney Island" previously appeared in the 2020 translation issue of *Pakn Treger*.

www.farlag.com

SAM LIPTZIN
She Sold Her Husband
And Other Satirical Sketches

Translated from the Yiddish by Zeke Levine

Farlag Press

CONTENTS

6	Landlords
14	The First Trip to Coney Island
18	The Aesthete: A Character Study
24	Rumes with Foynitshur
29	Elye Nu . . .
33	The Alrightnik
37	Business Before Pleasure!
41	When I Eat Fish
45	I Have No Luck!
49	Some Speaker!
53	He Wants a Car
58	The Babysitters
63	She Sold Her Husband
67	Company
71	A Twenty Pound Turkey
76	In the Hotel Kochalayn
81	Brighton Beach
87	A Good Time
92	The Battle Over a Ball
97	Cooling System
102	A Televi . . . shhh!
106	*Glossary*
109	*Translator's Postface*

Landlords

WHAT'S THAT? Not every landlord is the same? I agree! There are bad landlords, worse landlords, and downright disgusting landlords. But one thing you have to hand to them is that they are predictable: they look after their priorities and their first priority is ... demanding the rent! It seems that landlords, like bosses, are a diverse group—dogs with big ears and dogs with small ears.

Now let me tell you about my landlords in the places I've lived.

I'll start with my first landlord in Brownsville. Folks called him the "Semi-Jew" because he had half a beard.

Several legends surrounded his beard. Someone said that, back in the old country, a pogromist burned half of it off. Another said he was cursed by his grandfather because his father went around with *shikses*. A third suggested it was because he sat around all day scratching his chin, plotting how to buy up the whole block. These were all legends that were told.

But there's one story about that beard that's no legend. I heard he went to collect the rent from a neighbor one day and didn't give a receipt, then came back two days later demanding the rent again. The neighbor fainted from anger. Reaching for something so he wouldn't fall, he grabbed the landlord's beard, and that's how half the beard ended up in the tenant's hand, while the other half stayed on the landlord's face!

However the story went, before he was a landlord, he worked as a matchmaker, a bread baker, and a law-breaker. He pulled together enough money to throw up a few walls, built a house, and started knocking on doors asking for rent.

My second landlord was what you'd call "a gentleman." First, he came for the rent on the second, and second, he was simply a man who loved his tenants. There was not a month that he didn't come around with two black eyes from the neighborhood women on account of his great affection for them. I mean that when he came for the rent, he tried to kiss them. They didn't like this very much—such ungrateful tenants he had . . . I must say, sometimes a landlord isn't just a pig—he's an ass.

Now, my third landlord was a cultured man. When he came for the rent, he always carried off a couple of books. It seemed he was also somewhat musical because I once pulled three records out from under his coat—two Carusos and one Mischa Elman.

The fourth landlord was an outright crook—he could steal a man's socks right out of his shoes. The tenants had a good reason to keep silent when he came into the house—he could easily steal a gold tooth from the inside of your mouth.

My fifth landlord was, as we say, a family man. He'd come by when we were eating, and didn't wait to be invited in. If we said "come eat!" he'd sit down at the table—if we didn't say anything, he'd pull up a chair anyway. He was always trying to connect with his tenants. For example, he connected a pipe to one of his tenants' gas meter—so the tenant paid his bill. He did the same thing with the electric to a second neighbor. In this way, he became one with his tenants.

My sixth landlord, in the last place I lived, was an old bachelor—or as he was known around the neighborhood, "the old goat". The old goat was very stingy. When he came for the rent, he'd climb three or four steps at a time, to save his shoes and keep the stairs intact. Not to mention he didn't even trust himself, he'd count the bricks several times a day just to make sure, God forbid, nobody had pulled one out of the wall.

This landlord was also my tenant, he rented one of the four rooms that I rented from him . . .

He'd come for his money the first of the month, but if I asked for *his* rent on the third or fourth, he'd scream that

I was pressuring him.

Every month we had the same struggle. He'd insist that when I gave him the rent, he'd pay me my rent. I'd yell back that when *he* paid *my* rent, I'd give him his!

And so one fine day, this landlord ordered me to move out of all the rooms, and the next day, an officer came with a couple of guys and tried to throw me out. In the end, an officer threw all of my things into the street and I, with the others, threw out the landlord's stuff. In the evening, when the landlord came home, he was in for a surprise. The tenant committee was moving my stuff back into the rooms, and we threw him—the landlord—out in the street!

The First Trip to Coney Island

As soon as the greenhorn outfitted himself in a new American suit—with a crease down the pants—and managed to buy a watch with a gold chain from a peddler, his cousins took him out to see New York: theaters, concerts, parks, and even a trip to the zoo. They also decided to show him the famous amusement park, Coney Island.

Lovely Esther, one of the family, took one look at him and scoffed, "When Shepsl buys a new straw hat and throws away his boyish little cap, then I'll bring him out to a dance."

Shepsl answered, annoyed, "If my hat is the most important thing, maybe she should buy a hat and take it out dancing."

But, he thought it over for a while and reconsidered. And when another cousin told him that Saturday they would take him to Coney Island, he went out and purchased a nice new straw hat.

Saturday morning, Shepsl dressed in his new gray suit, put on his watch with the gold chain, as was worn back then: placed in a jacket pocket and with the ring of the chain pinned to the lapel. He combed his hair and put on, for the first time, his nice straw hat.

Eight of the family—cousins and friends—went with "Shepsl the Greenhorn" to Coney Island.

They traveled by streetcar, for a nickel, shlepping two or three hours.

On the way, the Americanized members of the family told Shepsl all about the wonderful and magical things they would see.

"There's Luna Park," said one cousin "Do you know what happens there? I don't need to tell you. You'll see for yourself soon enough."

Another cousin chimed in, "And what about Steeplechase? When we get on, you won't know if you're in the air or on the ground."

And Esther threw in her two cents: "There's nothing wrong with just walking around, hearing the excited screaming, seeing the 'little people,' seeing the girl who's half-human and half-fish, or winding through a dark tunnel in a little boat, where you might get a kiss," she laughed.

The longer they traveled, the more packed the streetcar got. Kids were hanging from the poles near the open windows. People stood one on top of the other. The bag of bathing suits dangled from one shoulder. The food they'd brought along got crushed, so that it started to smell. The streetcar smelled of roasted chicken, the odor of chopped liver filled the air, and the stuffed cabbage, which someone brought along in a glass jar, stung everyone's noses once the jar was smashed under somebody's foot.

Suddenly all the passengers caught the same scent: the foul smell of swampy water, and every face shone with happiness. All together, everyone started screaming. "Coney Island! Coney Island!"

A swarming ball of people pushed at the exits, trying to get themselves and their bags out, all the while looking for their group.

Finally, Shepsl the Greenhorn found his family. First, he glanced down at his watch: "How long was that ride?" But as he looked at his lapel, he could see that someone had torn his jacket—a pickpocket had cut the button hole—and the watch was gone, after such a short time.

The family tried to console Shepsl, assuring him he could have the jacket repaired, and he could always buy another watch from the peddler, since until he paid it off in full it was still insured.

Shepsl the Greenhorn was, at that moment, very disappointed with his first trip to Coney Island. But then they arrived at the bustling Surf Avenue and he heard the screams and saw people buzzing around him, buying "*ayz-krem*," sugar-wool ("*kottn-kendi*"), fresh popcorn and "*hot-dogs*."

Shepsl cast his eyes on all the wonders: the freaks, the half-naked dancers, the "six-hundred pound girl"—as they introduced her—and the "sixty-five pound Lilliputian," her husband.

The family got closer to Steeplechase, where a large inflated rubber lady greeted the crowd with hysterical laughter. Out front a man was sitting in a wire birdcage, selling tickets: a combination pass to twelve attractions for fifty cents.

Shepsl the Greenhorn cast his eyes on the other amazing sights: the swings, the horses, the ships, the Loop the Loop, and "the Stormy Glider," where you walked up five flights of steps, then slid down from the top in a kind of spinning bowl which wobbled like a fever patient.

The cousins, who remembered Shepsl's nickname in *kheyder*—"Shepsl the Daredevil"—wanted to see if the greenhorn was scared or not. They made their way over to the Glider, they climbed the steps—with Shepsl the Greenhorn right behind.

They all sat at the edge, and when somebody yelled "one, two, three" they all launched themselves at the same time.

The ride tossed them this way and that, but in the middle a stormy wind lifted the new straw hat off Shepsl's head. The hat went tumbling down. Yes, the straw hat arrived first . . . And when they landed at the bottom at full speed, they stepped all over the new straw hat, which was ground to shreds. Only the black band remained, hanging from one of the cousins' shoes—like a sign of mourning for the loss of the watch with the golden chain and the nice new straw hat.

Esther wanted to distract the greenhorn from all of the "pleasures" he'd experienced his first time in Coney Island. She invited him, even without a hat, to ride with her in the Tunnel of Love, where a little boat sailed through the darkness surrounded by brilliant panoramas. Playfully, they jumped into the boats, which followed one after the other and entered the tunnel.

Shepsl, who was very bashful, sat in the boat and waited for a suitable moment, or a word from Esther, for some encouragement to put his arm around her and give her a kiss.

But before he could get his bearings and make his move, the light returned and the boat came to a stop. The three minutes were up . . . As they exited the ride a rubber doll popped its head through a window and pointed at the passengers, with its long nose. Shepsl felt—and maybe Esther did too—that the long nose was aiming right at them.

Now, when Shepsl goes to Coney Island he recalls his first time there fifty years ago. He longs for his lost watch, for his lost hat, and for his lost kiss. But more than anything, he longs for the past fifty years!

The Aesthete: A Character Study

Introducing Mr. Drizzle: the Yiddishist, the culturist—the aesthete.

Does his fat belly catch your eye? He wants to show the world how ugly it is to gorge oneself on the feast. And so he pushes his stomach forward, urging the world: "You! Become a man! Become cultured!"

He doesn't carry a cane because of an injured leg, God forbid! He carries it because—as a popular writer advises his readers—every man must have something to lean on, above all such a fashionable cane. We must admit the dog—I mean, this "man of culture"—needs a stick to chew on, so why not such a regal-looking cane.

He doesn't wear the pince-nez glasses on his nose because he is blind, God forbid! He wears them because he wants to see the world better. In general, a man of culture without pince-nez is like a monkey without a tail: one might get the idea that he is simply a man . . .

You'll see this frequently: the Yiddishist-culturist puts on and takes off his glasses. Understand, he doesn't do this without reason. How do I explain? He wears the pince-nez on his nose, so he can see the world. He takes them off, so he can see what's happening under his nose.

Mr. Drizzle, as I have already explained, or tried to explain, loves culture—of course: this means proper culture, cooked kosher, in Yiddish.

For a more elegant phrase he will get up in the middle of the second act of a play, run home, and flip through the whole dictionary. Then the next morning he'll find the actor sitting in his corner seat at the cafe and explain: From now on, instead of the phrase "Rat bastard!" in the scene, use the more sophisticated expression "You wear a devil's crown upon your head."

Mr. Drizzle always carries around an intellectual brush, for the purpose of brushing and refining the human soul.

He is, as they say, an aesthete. To him, a proper tie is important, like proper manners. For example, eating herring, he says, with your hands is vile! As uncouth as eating meat stew and stuffed kishkes without a cruet of wine on the side. (Notice this beautiful, refined word "cruet").

Seeing a worker in his overalls sit down at the table is like seeing an English word in a Yiddish book without quotation marks around it. Such a misfortune causes him to lose weight.

So as you see, Yiddish "culture" has a very "high" meaning and therefore Mr. Drizzle engages often in "high society," in the "high world," on the "high chair." He is president of twenty-two societies, since the president's chair is always higher, and culture, he says, must always be elevated.

It's true that, from time to time, you'll find Mr. Drizzle in the underworld. But this is, in his words, for specific reasons. Culture must sometimes kneel down in order to lift up the underworld to a higher level

In case you happen to see Mr. Drizzle wrestling a rib-steak, holding the tail with his bare fingers, just know that in the evening Mr. Yiddish Culture will hold a lecture titled "Vegetarianism—The Goal of the Cultured Man," "Eating Meat: A Danger to the Evolution of Culture," or "Rib Steak, Culture, and Digestion." You see, Mr. Drizzle loves to base his arguments on facts.

Similarly, when you meet him at a wine-bar, with a blonde girl on his lap, you can be sure this is for the purposes of scientific research. That night you'll hear Dr. Drizzle speaking on "Love Between People," "Love for God and Love for Shikses," or "The Love of Jewish Culture by the Jewish People."

As I said, Dr. Drizzle loves to base his arguments on facts.

But woe be to Mr. Drizzle when he meets face to face with the proletariat. It hits him right in his eye like a stormwind. It seems a little dust in his eye causes tears to fall. "Of course," he says, "It's not so much the pain in my eye, but the nerve of the dust to meddle in the higher spheres and attack my pupil".

Look at our man Mr. Yiddish Culture when he walks by a picket line or workers' demonstration. His refined belly shrivels up. The pince-nez falls from his nose. His 260 pounds of culture lean on his cane to hear the 'coarse speech' of the commoners, in order to base his arguments on facts.

It doesn't bother him, he says, when people speak of revolution, as long as it's spoken delicately, but here he hears so many crude words in English, Spanish, and Chinese. Even those who speak Yiddish throw around such lowly English words as: "*sack,*" "*slack,*" "*unemployment insurance,*" "*crisis,*" "*speed up,*" "*rationalization,*" and other words that dishonor proper Yiddish speech.

Mr. Drizzle stands and shakes his cane, translating these words into refined Yiddish, only for himself. He grabs a dictionary from his pocket and saves Yiddish culture.

Nevertheless, he says, he loves to spend time with the proletariat. Their youth, he claims, "creates atmosphere" for his refined nose.

He comes to a proletarian meeting and meets a girl there. He tells her, "the panorama in this room, on the walls, does not create the proper mood."

"Mood from the walls?" laughs the girl, "Where do you come up with such nonsense? *No one's asking you to climb the walls.* We'll go down to the picket line, that's where the "mood" is."

"Picket, Picket, Picket", Mr. Drizzle chews over the words, "Let's sit and have a glass of water, and let's sing something, forget about the prosaic."

She looks at him and sits down.

Mr. Drizzle slips his belly under the table and peers with his oily eyes into the girl's mouth.

The girl bursts into song *"We are the builders"*... *"We build the future!"*

The middle-class aesthete is furious: "Future, shmuture! Sing a proper song"

The girl throws him a mean look, as he starts to sing: *"In veldl baym taykhl, dort zaynen gevaksn..."*

"Mister," laughs his acquaintance, "What are you? We are proletariats, fighters, Communists!"

"Me?" mustering up all the courage from his belly under the table. "I am a Yiddishist-culturist"

"Is that so?" the girl gives a laugh. "Does it pay well?"

"Strange people . . ." Mr. Drizzle loses his patience, "There are so many beautiful words in the world, like 'psychology', 'anthology', 'philology', 'geology', 'astronomy', 'physiology', 'Darwinism', 'Skepticism', 'Zionism.' The only word they like is 'Communism'— *Fe!*"

The girl sneers at the *Kulturnik* and hurries away.

Mr. Drizzle, the aesthete, knows exactly what to do in this situation. He pulls out his old-man handkerchief, wipes his blond mustache, and looks for another victim to torment with his refined words, speaking in arguments based on facts.

Rumes with Foynitshur

SO I GATHER you're talking about "*rumes*"? I swear, I wanted to marry off my son three years ago, but on account of a room—he's had to wait.

Meeting girls was easy for him. You know how it is, you can find ten girls for one boy, but rooms—there isn't one room for ten people!

I tell you, I have visited dozens of streets and floors and always hit a wall—I found no rooms.

So you'll understand how happy I felt when I discovered a family on our street was moving to a new city. I bought the husband a nice gift—as it was suggested to me—and asked him to keep his move a secret, like the Manhattan Project kept the atom bomb a secret. So I worked out a deal with the janitor and agreed to pay a 50 dollar fee for the rooms.

When I was finally able to take a look at the rooms, they were completely dark. I could hardly feel where there was a wall or a door . . . The woman from the apartment quickly let me know: "You have to take it as it is with the *foynitshur*, carpets, with the refrigerator, and even with those little Fascists—the cock-a-roaches that is." She told us we would have to pay $550 for the "convenience"

I thought to myself: I'll happily part with the money, as long as I can see my newly-wed son in a home of his own.

What can I say? As soon as my wife and I led my son to the *khupe*, I went out and bought a new set of furniture: everything from a washboard to a grater. And in order to rid the house of chometz, I called up a man who buys up old stuff. I thought to myself: it doesn't matter what he pays, as long as he empties out the apartment to make room for the new furniture.

The man came upstairs, gave a disapproving look, and told me, "your 'furniture' wouldn't even be good for a fire, because rotten wood doesn't burn, it only smokes."

But I thought: I must get rid of all this junk, the children need a home!

So I told him, "You know what, just take it. Bring your guys and carry it away."

But the man said to me, "What do you mean 'bring your guys?' When people carry away *foynitsur* they want to make some money. It'll cost you twenty-four dollars."

I decided: Well, if I'm already hanging from the gallows, I might as well stick out my tongue. So I told him: "Mister, bring your men and get to work."

So the man and his lifters came up the stairs and within an hour's time those carcasses were laid to rest in the basement.

I paid the few dollars and called for the janitor. "You can go ahead and "*peynt*" the "*rumes*." I told him what I had in mind: green for the kitchen, white for the frontroom, and tan for the bedroom.

He looked at me and laughed, "Why do you need to tell me your favorite colors? It's your money: choose the colors that suit you and do what you want."

Long story short, we found a couple of painters, and in two days the rooms were all painted white. Only when we took a look at the bill, we saw red. We paid them 78 dollars, and they weren't shy about helping themselves to the refreshments we'd put out. Even the gallon of liquor, which we were saving for the housewarming, disappeared before our eyes. What remained was an excuse: they thought, one of them insisted, that the bottle was paint thinner, so they poured the bottle out into the paint. Now, when the paint falls off the wall, there will be no explanation other than that the house is drunk . . .

All jokes aside, listen to the end of this sad story.

As soon as we brought the new furniture into the rooms, the janitor came and explained that there was no space for the old stuff in the basement, since the landlord had cleaned it up to rent it as a room. What can I say? I felt like I was going to faint. It seemed there was nothing I could do. But it finally occurred to me to get a few *boytshiks*, give them a quarter and ask them to bring the furniture out in the street. I certainly don't need to tell you, that for them—the young guys—it was a walk in the park. They hacked up and stacked up the furniture, fast and strong as an express train. It wasn't long before the gang had dragged everything from the basement out to the street.

As soon as we freed ourselves from our burden, we got a knock on the door. I opened up and saw a policeman. Without any pleasantries, he warned us to bring the furniture back into the house. He gave the club on his belt a spin, like he was the boss in the shop, and gave it to us straight: if the street wasn't cleared by the morning we'd all get new rooms—in prison.

In short, I ran down to the street, found the boys from before, gave them a few quarters, slipped them a book of matches and told them: "Burn this chometz that you see in front of you."

The gang took the quarters and the matches and before I could cross the street, the whole place was enveloped in smoke, thick black clouds that rose into the sky—it could make you believe we were standing in hell.

It wasn't long before I heard the bells and whistles of the firetruck, and became worried for myself. And the fear wasn't groundless. You see, I had to go right away to the courthouse to prove that I was no arsonist and had no intention of burning down the city.

In the stores the prices are on fire, and the landlords burn with resentment that they can only fleece you once—and they call me an arsonist? If I wasn't afraid of another court case I would say: "May all those dark rooms with their other '*bargains*' go up in flames—at least it would brighten things up!"

Elye Nu . . .

DON'T LOOK NOW. Here comes Elye Nu—let's move it so we don't get stuck with him. You'll end up missing lunch and you'll be so bored you'll faint.

Who is this Elye Nu? I'm actually surprised you don't know him already.

Elye Nu is a *landsman* and a neighbor.

What kind of name is Elye Nu, anyway? Well, it has a pretty simple meaning. It comes from the fact that everyone calls him Elye the Nudnik! But he doesn't give you the opportunity to call him by his full name, since he interrupts you in the middle. With half his name still hanging from your lips, you must be satisfied with only Elye Nu . . .

When you're sitting in the park on Sunday morning, immersed in a newspaper or a book, out of the corner of your eye you see Elye Nu, and with no indication or warning, he slaps you on the hand.

May God save us from such insanity. Imagine: it's a peaceful Sunday afternoon and you're sitting there with your full attention on the page, concentrating like a clock maker.

And Elye Nu wastes no time in reaching over to grab the newspaper or book from out of your hand, and laughing with a wild cackle:

"You can become cultured another time. For now, tell me, what's new in the world?"

And you want to answer him, "How can I tell you what's happening in the world, since you interrupted my reading—since you're such a nu . . ."

But Elye doesn't wait a beat. He starts telling you everything that's happening in the world.

"Yeah, and how's by you? Been making any bundles? It's not like back in the old days. Back then a 'bundle' meant something, and a good season could set you up for the entire year. But today it's different. It's like they say on the radio: it's all a big racket. Now it's just a shot on the machine and the bundle is ready. And what about next season? You've barely paid off your debts from yesterday, and you're already borrowing money for tomorrow."

"I dunno, people are talking about war. Is war good or bad? All I know is that after the last war my boss became extremely rich, a millionaire. He says that if the war lasts another three months, he'll give up the shop and go right to Wall Street."

"What do you say? Children, sons, soldiers? Praise God, my wife had three girls. No chance of them becoming soldiers . . . Yes, it's true, that an accident could happen—a bomb, for instance—even in the park."

On the tip of your tongue are the words "Yes, true, a bomb could go off in the park..." Elye Nu bombards your ears like a bomb. It's a great feeling, then, when your kid runs up, "We're ready to eat, Mom says come eat, because the food is getting cold."

But it often happens that Elye Nu comes by the house exactly at the moment you're eating. He's devised a strategy: when everyone's mouths are full of food, he has the chance to talk...

He speaks about everything under the sun. He sees people passing beef and chicken around the table, and this gives him inspiration:

"What can you say to the swindlers with their 'weights and measures'? It's frightening to walk into a store. Lately I don't let my wife go shopping. It's too easy to trick her. What do I do? I go alone, I haggle, we go back and forth ten times. But you ask, does it help? It does. I went out last week to go shopping for Shabbos. Meat, chicken, fish, and the other little odds and ends. I came home and showed my wife. She grabbed the piece of meat and screamed 'They gave you a good weight but it's all fat and bones. Where's the meat?' She looked at the chicken and laughed: "You call this a chicken? This looks like a dead rabbit..."

But Elye Nu didn't pause for laughter. He kept going with his story:

"And you know what else? What kind of swindlers, thieves, crooks they are? I went to them to change a twenty-dollar bill and they slipped me a fake ten dollar bill and a Canadian penny."

Even Elye's own wife talks about what a nu . . . he is:

Elye went with his wife to visit a sick friend. After he had made the patient sicker with all his talking, his wife told him it was time to go home. On the way his wife let him know how much of a nudnik he is. She told him "The sick man told me that, last time, you went to his place and stayed for three hours, and when you left, he felt saved!"

"If that's true," Elye Nu said, "I'll visit him more often—I'd do anything to save my friends!"

What do you think? Is Elye Nu waiting to pounce on his next victim? Run as quickly as you can!

The *Alrightnik* . . .
(Dedicated to the Marshall Plan)

IF YOU HAVEN'T already met my father-in-law, Mr. Shmilik Feterman, I think you should get to know him. He's a man who wears his hat pushed back, so you can clearly see the golden pince-nez glasses sitting on his nose. He carries his silver tobacco box facing away from you, but he's always ready to treat you to a bit of the stuff. But as soon as others around him start sneezing, my father-in-law sneezes as well, so that everyone will say "Bless you!" and buy more handkerchiefs from him.

My father-in-law is not a man who can simply live without calculations. On the contrary: he turns everything over in his head and calculates: even when they don't add up, there are still calculations in his head.

My father-in-law has a plan for everything, and I became an active part of one of those plans. That's why he's now my father-in-law, which is not an easy situation to be in.

He had a daughter he wanted to marry off, and someone told me about the match. When the matchmaker brought me to their wealthy home, I wondered why so many different-colored lamps were burning—green, blue, and yellow—all these colors made me dizzy. I asked my dear father-in-law: why are the lights so dim in the house? He responded, "Atmosphere." He loves beauty.

The second time, I went to meet his daughter alone. She also kept things dark. When I asked, "Why do you keep the house so dark?" She responded, "In the dark our eyes will shine."

A couple of darkened weeks, through all their dinners and parties until—we were married.

The day after the wedding, when I lit up the house properly—that's when things went dark. My "soul-mate" had pockmarks all over her face, warts on her nose, cataracts in her eyes, and a "golden smile"—fourteen false teeth.

I quickly realized—my father-in-law's plans worked...

My father-in-law also builds houses, all to a plan, and he does this—just as he'd assured the matchmaker—merely for one reason: to help the poor, so they would have a place to lay their heads. But as soon as someone wants to move into a house, my father-in-law asks one thing: sign this document—that's all he asks for in return for his kindness. Now, you must go through him to rent the vehicle transporting the furniture to the house, and also you must go through him to rent the vehicle to bring the furniture from that place to another. He raises the rents frequently. If someone wants to move out of their place, they must pay such a hefty transportation fee that it's not worth the trouble. The tenant either has to pay the price or leave all their furniture and possessions with my father-in-law.

My father-in-law also gives loans to help poor businessmen—also with a plan. He believes, he says, in helping people to improve their condition. He said once to Pesye the Widow:

"You've inherited a great store, but you have nothing to put in it. I can give you stock, clean the windows, give you good publicity—I just need to recoup the capital. That's all I want."

"Here's my plan," says my father-in-law. "One of my sons is very talented, I will make him the manager—that's it. Since he is my son, it's a little beneath him to work for someone else. So please sign the store over in his name . . ."

And what can I tell you? Pesye the Widow—may she rest in peace—was quickly "helped" by my father-in-law's plan.

Of course, if you know my father-in-law, you should also know my mother-in-law. Honestly, my mother-in-law has nothing much to say: she just goes along with all of my father-in-law's plans. And whenever he has to complete a task that he feels is beneath him, he asks his wife and she spreads her "gifts" around the city, so that people become excited before even unwrapping the "present."

And my father-in-law has a cousin, somewhere in France—Madame Blumky is her name. She also has a son, a "proper" young man, lanky as a broom, and mean as the devil. My father-in-law had a plan to set him up with Frances, a woman who had been betrayed and deserted by her husband.

What do you think my mother-in-law did? She went along with the plan, knocking on doors and gates, to let everyone know that the clumsy devil would make the best father for Frances's children. And my father-in-law combed his beard, cleaned himself up, preparing himself to dance at the wedding...

My father-in-law is a great philanthropist, but you know that already. If he's working from a plan, it's not for him—it's for the whole world. And if my father-in-law gives away a chair at the Eastern Wall, and another behind the Torah, it's not because he has some ulterior motive. No, it's simply that he's got a plan...

But if you decide not to go along with his plans, I wouldn't want to be in your shoes. He'll tip his tophat and give a nudge with his cane and say:

"Hey, my fellow working men, respect your Uncle Shmilik and his gold chain."

Business Before Pleasure!

WHY DO YOU HESITATE, fool? Come, warm up with me! I'm fresh and young. You don't know what the five fingers mean? *Five bucks* . . . five dollars, understand? Don't look at me with just one eye! You won't be able to see me well . . . you see a girl? A model, a real gem I'm telling you . . .

So what if I'm a street-walker, what about it? Don't you know that we, prostitutes, are the most decent people in the world? Ha-ha-ha . . . We are always open-hearted, and don't hide from our sins. And what makes me sinful anyway? Because I sell my body? And you, fool, don't sell your hands to the shop? I also wanted to sell my hands—I went around for months looking for work—and no luck!

And the doctor doesn't sell his soul? And the professor really has a clean conscience? And the writer has a pure heart? And the manufacturer, the banker, and the store-owners, are blameless lambs, are they? I sell myself. myself. You like me? Fine! You don't? *Good-bye!*

You know them, the ones with their fancy top-hats? I know them! They've sold their souls!

Congressmen, senators, diplomats—they trade in conscience like they're selling bagels in the street. People sell their souls like the hides of skinned cattle. Everything is a business! There's a market for everything! Buying, selling! *Five bucks, please* . . . I am a part of this business world, not a Rockefeller, not a Ford, but I am on the market. I can still compete . . .

> *I am a pretty girl*
> *My mama calls me Molly*
> *I give away just one wink*
> *Everyone comes running*

I have a little boy. He tells me that when he grows up, he's going to be a judge. A judge, an honest man, a noble judge. Just today, the judge freed me for the eighteenth time. I am, he says, not guilty. Not guilty, ha-ha-ha . . . Not guilty and pure, like the judge himself . . .

Earlier I had myself a little drink and cried a lot. Any time I recall the past, I cry. He stands before me, my first love, and this is what he looked like: dark black hair, eyes like fiery coals, tall and elegant. In the War he was a corporal. He received medals for his heroism, and in the end—he fell like a fool.

His general invited me to see him, to give me the medals my lover had earned. We ate together, drank and passed the time . . . then he told me he wanted nothing more to do with me. Now I pass from hand to hand.

You laugh at me? I'm not drunk! You can understand me clearly! I am intelligent! I went to school! I have an education! My mother hoped I'd be a doctor .... but I loved music. I can sing. I can sing in key ...

> *My love, my love*
> *I always sit and wonder*
> *When will the sun shine for me*
> *And cast away the dark night?*

Hey! You cheapskate. Why don't you clap for me? When I worked in the cabaret, everyone applauded me!

I can work. I've worked in a restaurant; the boss loved me, so his wife sent me away ... I have also worked as a book-keeper in a shop, and the foreman loved me. He was a disgusting old man, with a sparse prickly mustache. And since I wouldn't kiss him, he sent me away.... *Come on! Business before pleasure!*

I am now like the judge, like the policeman, like Rockefeller, like Ford. If it's business, let's do business. *Come on boys!*

Preachers, priests, bankers—compared to you I am an angel! You are my fiercest rivals. Ha-ha-ha! Come challenge me here in the streets! Ha! a cruel joke ...

> *Don't pray for me any longer*
> *In church or in shul*
> *Your speech sounds to me*
> *Like a dog's howl*

You gather around me and amuse yourself with my speech. I've become entertainment for this dirty crowd. One gets pleasure from my body, another from my chatter.

But I'm not chattering. I'm exposing my broken heart—the wounds I remedy with schnapps, like iodine for a cut...

I'm not the prostitute—It's you who surrounds yourself with pimps and parasites.

From pimps to hypocrites, they're all partners in the same business: they all make their livelihood from my blood...

I want to be equal with all people, for people to accept me as their own!

You laugh at me. You don't believe me? I spit on all of you—rotten people... you've all sold your souls!

When I Eat Fish

YOU'LL HAVE to excuse me. When I'm eating, I don't like conversation—and I have my reasons. When I eat, I eat.

Understand? Joking around, gossiping, playing cards, fighting, these are all good when you're in a group. But when I eat, I want to eat.

I won't answer you at all, even if you talk to me from morning to night. But don't think that a word from me is some kind of rare treasure. And if you think I don't have anything to say in reply, you're making a grave error. It's just that I have, once and for all, decided that I can't do two jobs at once. When I speak, I speak. When I eat, I eat.

In fact, this has been my custom my entire life. I go out to eat when others have finished eating. And when I go to a restaurant, I find a table somewhere in the corner, sit down like I'm the only person on Earth, and—eat. Since, if I'm eating, I eat!

And I especially like to be alone when I eat fish. For a bit of good fish I'd give you heaven and earth. For some pike, especially, I'd give you my piece of the World to Come— my seat in Eden. And if you're a stubborn negotiator I might even throw in the whole World to Come, just leave me the Leviathan . . .

When I eat, I'm as quiet as the piece of pike on my plate. Like I said, when I eat, I eat!

Recently I went to a cafeteria, looked around the pots and pans and noticed that the cook had put aside a platter of fresh, hot pike. The fragrant steam leaked from the fish's mouth—he looked like he'd only just jumped out of the water onto dry land.

What can I tell you? I grabbed the plate of fish, looked for a corner and, as always, sat down alone.

I got up to get to the horseradish and . . . Oh, great! wonderful! *L'Chaim*! Motl Serenude is here.

As Motl pulled his sweaty hand away from our greeting, he picked a bit of white bread from the slice that was sitting on my plate, started rolling it up in a small ball and expressed his happiness about seeing me.

"I would"—he said—"sooner expect to meet my great-grandfather—rest his soul—than to see you in a restaurant."

In short, Motl Serenude started to talk, tell stories, ask questions, and all as I was in the middle of eating.

I'll tell you frankly, I'd only wish upon the worst antisemite, that he should be in the middle of eating fish, with a mouth full of bones and be forced to answer Motl Serenude.

Imagine: you've had a fish bone stuck in your gums, another between your teeth, you're about to choke on a third, and then you hear Motl Serenude yell out:

"What do you have to say about that?"

And this time he had picked out some especially fascinating questions! And since I didn't answer him quickly, given the fish bones stuck in my mouth, he triumphantly banged on the table:

"Ha-ha" he laughs. "You got fish swimming around in there? Well? Say something!"

And as quickly as I put a bit of hard bread in my mouth to dislodge the bone, which is apparently mounting an uprising in my mouth, he got in another question...

"What do you think they'll do," he asked, "if they catch the bank-robber alive?"

To tell the truth, I had no idea what to answer him. Honestly, the fish-bone that had snuck its way between my teeth and kept poking my tongue was more intriguing to me than his question.

Motl Serenude had another victory over me, and so dropped another gem: "Do you think someone will come up with a patent for a submarine that flies like an airplane?"

I wanted to say, "You, ox, you jackass, you bonehead, why do you insist on bothering the hell out of me?" I'm eating a fish, a pike, with bones on every side, why can't you just let me eat? When I'm eating fish—I like to eat!

But it's polite to chat a while, when you're not choking on a fish's ribs. But I started to choke—really choke—so that my eyes popped out like my fish's ...

My ears continued to hear questions. Questions, opinions, and foolishness, from this man, who couldn't answer any questions himself!

What can I tell you?—It didn't turn out well for me. My fish remained on the table while I had to be rushed to the hospital! The only way I could settle things with Motl Serenude was, when he came to see me in the hospital, I begged the doctor to run some tests on him, on his intelligence that is.

From then on, it's been a custom—what am I saying, a custom?—a law! a strict law: when I eat, I eat! I tell you, that I won't answer a word in reply, you won't distract me. I came to eat. And when I come to eat, I eat!

I beg you, please don't be a Motl Serenude. God willing, when we finally have the antisemites locked up, we will feed them pike, carp, and hedgehogs, and all the Motl Serenudes of the world will sit around the table—like an interrogation—and they'll just ask questions and demand answers.

But what have you got against me? Let me eat in peace! For me, as I eat, I eat! I will not answer a single word! I'll be as silent as the fish ... Oy! I've got another bone in my throat!

I Have No Luck!

WHEN PEOPLE SAY that for everything you need a little luck, they know what they're talking about.

Respectable people have *policies:* fire policies, policies protecting them from theft, sickness, and even death.

On top of that, people buy policies for laying in the hospital, policies for operations, and even policies for accidents, i.e. in case something should befall you—if you fall on something, or if something falls on you . . .

There are people who protect their eyes, their hands, their voice, and even their false teeth.

So what does this have to do with me? I'm referring to the fact that I have no luck.

For years we had a fire policy. One day I was talking to a neighbor about fires, and he joked: "What are you scared of? Your house will never burn, since rotten things never burn. And with your poverty, the insurance company won't give you a hand, they'll just give you the finger."

I told myself that my neighbor must know what he's talking about, so when it came time to renew the policy, I ignored it and didn't bother to pay.

A few months later, a fire broke out at my neighbor's place. The fire burned up a few houses on the block—mine included.

My neighbor collected a nice check and immediately started talking about building an even bigger house. And I didn't even earn that finger—I have no luck...

My father-in-law had a life insurance policy. Over the years, he had paid in quite a handsome sum. Suddenly he realized that he was throwing his money away. He was torturing himself to pay for a policy, and what would it be worth after his death? So he ended the policy—and stopped paying.

Not even two years went by, and he was sick from head to toe. We spent every penny on his health—and then, he went ... We got no inheritance and had to pay for the funeral.

Some people I know get lucky. A *landsman* of ours bought life insurance—he paid into it for only one year—then he was gone ... I don't know what heaven he found himself in, but his wife is now sitting in seventh heaven with her own stack of money. Now she's looking for a new husband to help her raise her nest egg!

Like I said, some people have good luck. I belong to three organizations that keep me covered. I belong to a society that pays sick-benefits. As soon as someone is sick for a week, the society pays benefits for the second week. I belong to the union; the union pays for the third week, and contributes to the cost of medications.

God help me, one day I got sick. I decided, once and for all: I wanted to see what the organizations would do for me. I wanted to know what I get for my money.

In short, I went to the hospital. This was on a Friday. They gave me some pills, an examination and everything else necessary. "And now," the doctor says, "you can eat a good Friday dinner and tomorrow—Shabbos—you'll have a fine day of rest. You must rest well."

To tell you the truth, the pills and other medications worked well and quickly, and I made a speedy recovery.

But lying in the hospital, I learned that sickness is a healthy business—it pays for itself . . .

A patient explained to me that since he'd been sick, he had actually gotten closer to a little bit of health. Earlier, no one had paid any attention to him, and now they're looking in his mouth . . . he got health benefits from four societies; from the shop—benefits, from the union—benefits.

A second patient told me that he had been in the hospital for eight weeks, and he often felt that he was on vacation: They bring him food, they wash and clean him. He either goes for walks all day, or he lies in bed and watches television. The only difficulty, he says, is that he can't leave the hospital. He can't walk down the street and eat a pastrami or salami sandwich, and he can't drink a beer.

What I'm really trying to say is—you have to have luck.

Once I'd been in the hospital for a week, the doctor told me I was healthy and said I could go right back to work...

And I told myself: I pay my hard earned dues to the organizations, to the union, to the societies, and before you know it, I am healthy—no benefits, no medicine, no flowers, no candies...

The doctor understood how I felt and joked: "What do you want? For your few dozen dollars I should make you sick?'"

As you see, I have no luck...

Some Speaker!

THE LADIES' AUXILIARY decided to host a "cultural evening." The question was, who should be the guest speaker? The chair of the organization quickly put forward Dr. Loeb as the best speaker—he is a *vonderful man* with *personality*—and everyone agreed. But a second question arose: how do we get an audience? This was met with a flurry of suggestions.

The secretary suggested organizing a banquet. With a banquet, she pointed out, they would be guaranteed success. Lectures can't always be "digested," but food, she claimed, with garlic, and a knish, a noodle kugel—the men would not be able to resist . . . and the women wouldn't hate it either.

The finance secretary jumped up and yelled "*I don't like benkwits*! They cost too much and don't give me any pleasure. My husband *soffers* from ulcers—I wouldn't wish this fate upon any of you—he gets them after knishes and *pudding*! I propose an *amendment*, we should arrange a dance. *Everybody likes a dence!*"

"Come off it! You're talking nonsense!" the chairwoman protested. "These days, if you want to *draw a crowd*, the *best ting is to arrange a kard parti*. With a *kard parti*, you can be sure that everyone will come. We'll start with a little fun, and after that they'll enjoy a *lekshure*.

"I propose a *sobstitushon*"—voices erupted from around the room.

When the chairwoman asked who was in *favor*, hands shot up.

By three in the afternoon, it was clear that the evening would be a success . . . a few tables, with groups around them, were already busy—that is, during the day, when they were playing all kinds of *games*. In the evening the men appeared, and divided into groups—a group to play poker, and a group to play pinochle.

Around 8:00 the hall was packed with men, women, and children. Everyone had chosen their company, their table, and their game.

At 8:30, when the speaker, Dr. Loeb, came into the room, one of the players, not knowing who it was, threw a few words his way:

"*Mister*, you came too late, all the tables are full . . ."

"I am the speaker," Dr. Loeb replied in a flustered voice.

"Oh! This is the man for the *cultural part*!" a woman called out.

Another yelled to the chairwoman of the Lady's Auxiliary, Mrs. Katkin: "The man with the *kultural* is here!"

Mrs. Katkin ran up to Dr. Loeb, grabbed his briefcase, brought him a chair and started to explain:

"*You see*, in order to have a big crowd, we arranged a card party, and as soon as Mrs. Gold comes—you see—Mrs. Gold has a *beauty parlor*, she closes her business at 10, and without her we can't start the *cultural part*."

The chairwoman, Mrs. Katkin, looked over at the table, to see what was going on. And asked Mr. Loeb, what game he played . . .

"You can play a hand, until Mrs. Gold arrives."

Dr. Loeb smiled: "I have studied many things, but cards—this is something my head cannot grasp."

Dr. Loeb pulled out a newspaper to read, and Mrs. Katkin apologized and ran back to the table to pick up her hand.

Sitting at the table, Mrs. Dvorkin glanced over at Dr. Loeb and with pity noticed him sitting all alone. She gathered up the courage to speak up to the chairwoman, Mrs. Katkin:

"You must invite the doctor over to our table. We can make room for a sixth"

"*Yes,*" Mrs. Katkin agreed, "I'm *smart* like you, and asked him already, but, you think that a doctor knows everything? He can't just pick up some cards, just try and make him!"

Mrs. Dvorkin burst out laughing: "*Some speaker!*"

He Wants a Car

HIS WHOLE LIFE LONG Mr. Broido worked with machines. He started his career as an operator on a foot-pedal-operated-machine. In a second shop he learned to stoke the furnace to make the machines run. Some time later, the shop changed over to treader-operated machines. Finally, he became the operator of a machine powered by electricity.

Every machine sucked the marrow from Broido's bones, and, standing on his feet all day in the shop, he felt that he no longer had legs—just stumps.

In his old age, Broido decided to buy a car—a machine of his own. "If," he says, "I have to sit all day breaking my back behind the machine at work, I should have a machine that will give my stumps a ride back home. And it will, of course, be good for my sciatica and my lower back pain, since I won't have to drag myself onto the subway, running up and down the stairs."

When Mr. Broido made the choice to buy a car, he kept the idea locked away in his head. He wanted to surprise his wife, his kids, and most importantly—his grandchildren.

He daydreamed about everyone squeezing into the car: he and his wife in front, at the wheel. He loved his Rosalie dearly, and wanted her right next to him—he wanted to share this great pleasure with her. However, he thought, Rosalie had a habit of 'taking the wheel' herself. If he wanted to turn right, she'd tell him to turn left. If he went through the park, she'd want to take the drive, so he determined that they would sit in the front, but with their grandson Herschel between them. "I hate backseat—and passenger seat—drivers," he said to himself.

He also had to consider how the rest of the family would be arranged: in the back, his three daughters with their babies on their laps, two son-in-laws in the trunk, and the third... Well, he was sure there'd always be someone who wouldn't want to come and could stay home.

When Broido had figured out the seating arrangements, there remained the question of what type of car to buy. A Ford reminded him of a *ferd*—a horse. And a Buick?—would make people think he was riding a *bik*—a goat! And the Kaiser Frazer—what's with the rhyme? It sounds like a children's song.

So he took his wooden feet down to a car dealership, and got acquainted with some of the cars.

When the salesman gave him a wink, asking whether he wanted a car with butter, or without—it took him some time to digest what this meant. But he finally understood that "with butter" means—"greased." Broido realized it wasn't the car that would be greased—but the salesman's palms.

Mr. Broido let him know directly that he was a good union man, who didn't stand for bribes. He fought this sort of "*grafting*" in the union bureaucracy, so he can't travel any further down this road.

To get rid of him the salesman gave him a little booklet containing all the necessary instructions for learning the rules and regulations around driving a car. And with a devilish wink he said that they'd let him know by mail when the car was ready for him.

Mr. Broido took his learning seriously. If he was going to be driving a car—especially with his wife and kids in it—he wanted to know everything to do with cars and driving, how to stay safe and obey the law ...

He took the booklet to the shop, and read it at work, during his lunch-break, and on his commute home. He studied all the time, especially at home. Instead of washing the dishes and spending time with his family as usual, Mr. Broido sat in a corner with his little book in hand and immersed himself, conducting experiments and exercises, turning his hands, putting his hand out, pushing down with the right foot, pushing down with the left foot, climbing up on the seat, a finger up, a finger toward himself, a push, a wave, a ride.

This is how he spent most evenings. His family got the feeling that something wasn't quite right with him. When he was absorbed in his exercises and mumbling to himself, Rosalie and the children would hide in the kitchen behind the cabinets, and with fearful eyes follow his act.

"We've lost him!" his faithful wife Rosalie exclaimed to their neighbor.

Her neighbor calmed her down: "Don't be a fool! You have to look at what he's reading, I wouldn't be surprised if, in his old age, he's started reading romance novels . . . You can't put anything past men," the neighbor advised confidently. "I had the same thing with my husband"

Weeks went by this way. As quickly as he learned a chapter of the book by heart, he forgot another, and as many times as he knocked on the salesman's door to get the car, nothing helped. He just kept putting him off day after day.

Mr. Broido was very annoyed that he had to keep learning and revising every day, until doing exercises and muttering to himself became second nature.

One evening, when he lay down exhausted from his work, he started driving in his sleep, turning the steering wheel in his hands and braking with his feet, and all the while his family looked on terrified. A shaken Rosalie called out to one of her children: "Quick! Call an ambulance, bring a doctor!"

The ambulance soon arrived, siren blaring, and stopped abruptly outside the door.

Mr. Broido fitfully opened his eyes and ran to the window. He saw a beautiful, shining vehicle at the front door. "Children!" he called out, "grab your mother and come quick. I got the car, I want to take you out on the first ride!"

The Babysitters

THE SOSKINS had dreamed for a while now about going to hear a great concert. They both loved music and spoke often about the times they would wait in line for hours just for a place to stand at a fine opera.

They—man and wife—were both shop-workers whose earnings were miserable: they couldn't even consider seated tickets. They had fantasized that, after their wedding, better times would come. They could go more often to concerts, to the opera, and maybe even afford a seat.

After they married, they had a child, a feisty little one, who liked to put on his own "concerts." His solos were heard down the entire street. He was especially famous for his midnight performances.

The Soskins forgot about going out to concerts and operas. Their house was full of song: either the parents were singing their child to sleep, or the child "sang" his own songs. So the Soskins were quite happy to hear about a concert organized by their friends from the old country. Finally, they would have a chance, after a long year's hiatus, to listen to music, catch some new songs and see their friends.

But now they had a problem: who could watch the kid? Mrs. Soskin thought about her mother. She knew her mother loved the child and would be happy to play with her grandson and put him to bed, rather than sitting at home alone.

Mr. Soskin quickly reminded his wife that her mother didn't have any desire to spend the night at their house, since she liked only her own bed. Instead he would ask his father to be a "*babysitter*"—to sit an evening with the child at their house.

This time it was Mrs. Soskin who reminded her husband that his father would not want to come to spend the night. True, she admitted, he loved their child and home, but it was not religiously observant enough for him: The doorways without mezuzahs, the dishes mixed, the food not kosher enough.

"Tell you what," He tried to reassure her, "We will promise to bring them home at the end of the night—either your mother or my father—whoever agrees to be a babysitter for the evening.

Mrs. Soskin talked it over with her mother. The old mother hesitated slightly: it would be difficult for her, but she finally admitted that sometimes you have to go out and see the world.

"Go on then. I'll just get to bed a few hours later than usual."

Mr. Soskin, wanting to be completely sure they were covered, had a talk with his father.

His father gladly accepted. "Wonderful!" His grandson was the apple of his eye. And in order not to get bored, he decided to bring along a book of psalms in his pocket. The evening would be a double joy: singing psalms and being a babysitter.

When Mr. and Mrs. Soskin had cleaned up to get ready for the concert, the elder Mr. Soskin arrived with the book of psalms in his pocket. He embraced his grandson warmly, then sang a little melody to amuse the child and to give the Soskins a chance to continue getting dressed and cleaned up.

When they were ready to go, Mrs. Soskin realized that she'd forgotten to call her mother to tell her that she didn't need to come, and now it was too late.

Mr. Soskin quickly solved the problem. He asked his father, when Mrs. Soskin's mother came to the house, if he would thank her and ask her to go home. She could be the babysitter another time.

As soon as the Soskins left the house, the grandmother arrived. At first, she was annoyed that she'd traveled so many blocks for nothing, but as soon as her grandson hugged her, grabbed her nose and started playing with the medallion on her chest, her face shone with happiness and she forgot all about going home.

She sat down on the sofa by the baby's crib and began to sing a little lullaby—a lullaby she used to sing to her own daughter to put her to sleep.

The old grandfather, after pacing around a while with his book of psalms, humming a tune, sat down on the sofa next to his in-law.

Both looked through the railing of the child's crib and looked upon their grandson's beaming face.

As if of one mind, they began to talk practically about their children and the future of their grandchild.

In the low light the two looked each other in the eyes. For the entire time they had been in-laws, they never had the opportunity to talk this much—they talked about their love for their children and got to know each other well too.

The hour was late and the grandmother grew tired. She remained seated, bundled up in the corner with her head lowered. The grandfather attempted to leaf through a few psalms, but the pages got stuck between the fingers of his sleepy hands.

A fine "duet" graced the quiet of the night. The grandfather snored and whistled through his nose, and the grandmother accompanied this with a weak cough, and from time to time with a sudden moan . . . and they lay their tired heads one against the other.

The child woke up, and realizing his mother was not around, began to cry.

At midnight the Soskins came home happy and smiling, with silent songs still on their lips. They unlocked the door and both let out a hearty laugh.

The two *babysitters* didn't even hear the door opening. They slept peacefully and carried on their "concert" of snoring, whistling, and coughing. The child, on the other hand, was awake, sitting up, and watching over his grandparents—now he was the "babysitter" for the evening.

She Sold Her Husband

THERE WAS A "COLD WAR" UNDERWAY at the Rivkins' house. Mr. Rivkin complained constantly about the frosty reception he received when he came home from work, that the dinner on the table was always cold as ice, and that Mrs. Rivkin never talked to him unless it was about traveling to Lakewood in the winter, where she loved to watch children skating. And the only warmth she ever offered him was a choice between iced-coffee or ice cream soda.

But when Mrs. Rivkin spoke about her husband with others, it was all sweetness and light. She lived by the policy: "Don't air your dirty laundry in public," especially when she was talking with Mrs. Brand.

Mrs. Rivkin smelled something with her female nose: her husband's weakness for Mrs. Brand. He always had something nice to say about her latkes and hot borscht, which he sometimes ate at her house when Mrs. Rivkin was out in the country.

Mrs. Brand, however, was not too enthusiastic about Mr. Rivkin. It seemed she had "studied" him thoroughly, so she knew his weaknesses. She knew that he was stingy, not just in terms of money, but also with his compliments: with every kiss must also come a pinch. So she knew that he was not only a stingy man, but a bitter one at that.

Mrs. Rivkin tried to sell her husband's positive attributes to Mrs. Brand, advertising a "great product." Her method was that of all great businesspeople, extolling the product's virtues to the skies.

"When my husband comes home all dreamy," Mrs. Rivkin explained in an innocent tone, "I know he's thought up a new subject for a poem. My husband hates to brag, but you really should hear him read some of his poems. He can come home, sit quietly for an hour or two, then you can hear some beautiful words—a real song! Have you heard my husband sing? When he sings in the house, birds perch on the fire escape to listen."

Mrs. Brand shrugged and continued listening to the impassioned speech Mrs. Rivkin was making about her husband.

"You think that I love him for nothing? No, there are good reasons—he deserves it. When other men sit around dealing cards, paying no attention to their wives, playing and losing their meager couple of dollars, my husband is sensible, he saves for a rainy day . . . What more do you need? When my husband gives a kiss, he puts his entire heart and soul into it. I feel vibrations like music, like a warm voice echoing in the forest. You see this bruise," Mrs. Rivkin points, "This is an echo, the vibration of a loving kiss...."

Mrs. Brand was enchanted by Mrs. Rivkin's high praise, and all of this passion for her own husband. Mrs. Brand thought for a moment and cursed herself that she was so uncultured not to appreciate the beautiful soul of Mr. Rivkin.

She convinced herself that this was the reason he sat around her place for hours, but never said a word, only muttered under his breath. He was such a creative man, and he expressed his love through poetry. But her simple mind just couldn't grasp it.

Yes, she remembered, just the other day she had seen a few birds by the window, when he was sitting on the couch, and tried to kiss her . . . Mrs. Brand could have simply kicked herself for treating Mr. Rivkin so badly, for pushing him away when he tried to kiss her . . .

After a few such intimate, "friendly" conversations between Mrs. Rivkin and Mrs. Brand, Mr. Rivkin noticed that Mrs. Brand was paying him ever warmer attention, while the war in the Rivkin household got ever colder.

Finally the day came that Mr. Rivkin left his home and his wife, and went away to live with Mrs. Brand.

Mrs. Rivkin felt pleasantly relieved that the Cold War had finally ended and she was free of that terrible man.

A while later, when Mrs. Rivkin saw Mrs. Brand, she asked her warmly, as if nothing had transpired: "Well, how are things in your new life? Has Mr. Rivkin written any new poems? I am sure," she winked, "that your home is now full of song."

"Yes, well," Mrs. Brand answered, slightly ashamed, "He doesn't sing quite like a bird, and I'm stuck in a cage!"

Company

DON'T COMPLAIN that you live on the fifth floor. It's true that the seltzer-man, the grocery-man, and the butcher don't want to bring your orders up that high, and you yourself have to catch your breath whenever you climb "up to the heavens." Your heart beats like a drum, but that's nothing compared with some other troubles.

But listen to what Mrs. Berson—the woman that lives on the first floor—has to say. If she doesn't die young, it will only be because she's already past forty. And if she has any strength left at all, it's also thanks to her youth.

Mrs. Berson lives with her husband and children in an apartment of four rooms. But thanks to all that space her home has become something of a hotel. The Bersons are lovely people by nature. They love company, hosting guests, meeting neighbors, and in general, anyone who has something difficult to talk about drops by the Berson's on the first floor.

Early in the morning, as the Bersons turned on their radio to hear the latest from the weatherman, Mr. Lachman, from the fifth floor, came running in like the wind. He'd already rang the doors of the Rosenblums and the Lubins. He also liked company. He just wanted it to be cheerful, so he called everyone over to the Berson home.

"You understand," he explained, "I am the only person in my house, and on the fifth floor no less—that's a long way to go! Going to the grocery store, carrying everything up, then making myself a cup of coffee—it isn't worth it. And really, what kind of taste does that leave in my mouth, sitting by myself and drinking coffee? See, with company it's something else altogether. With company I make more than one cup, and drink it enthusiastically. And who can even speak when trying a piece of Mrs. Lubin's fish, or Mrs. Rosenblum's marinated herring!"

When Mrs. Berson offered him a third cup of coffee, he answered with his signature response: "How could I say no?"

By the evening, you see, things were already hopping in the Berson household. But at that moment, Mr. Shain came by for a conversation about art and music; Mr. Kuprin dropped in because his wife wanted quiet so she could listen to *The Yiddish Hour*; and Mr. Pinchuk, the widower, came around to kill a few hours, since he had nothing else to do.

The surrounding neighbors knew that the Bersons' place was always lively; there was always company over. You'd hear a new joke, and on top of that there was sure to be Mrs. Berson's strudel and her *birobidzhankes*, a type of honey-dough—a pleasure to put in your mouth. Then Mr. and Mrs. Greber would come from the building next door, and they brought along the Gureviches, and Shreiberman, and—who didn't they bring?

If it occurred to Mr. Berson to say that he wanted to go to a movie, a discussion would break out about the movie: "Good! Bad!" People talk, people would talk for so long, that the movie would be over—and the theater would be closed. The evening ended with a suggestion from Mr. Lachman to put on a fresh pot of coffee.

Of course, along with the coffee comes everything that can be found in the refrigerator, and with that songs of praise from the guests. "The strudel," says Pinchuk, "is heavenly!" Mr. Shain relished the chopped liver, and Mr. Shreiberman is too busy devouring the vegetarian salad—so he has no chance to say anything, but his eyes speak for him. In the end, when Mr. Berson gets up the next morning to get ready for work and wants to pack something for lunch in the shop—he finds the fridge empty as a hollow eggshell.

The best, though, is when Mr. Berson turns his radio on to a classical station. Before he can even catch a note from the orchestra, one of the regular guests comes knocking at the door. Before anything, the guest runs over and turns off the radio, then begins to complain: "I ran from the house, because my kids made me nervous with the nonsense they play on the radio. Then I come to you—grown adults—and you're being foolish with the radio just like the kids!"

Plus, don't forget, the first floor has many advantages. It's a good way station for the neighbors on the higher floors. One woman wanted a warm bottle of milk for her child, so she came around to the Bersons'. A second woman carried a bag of clean laundry up from the basement, but in the middle realized she wanted something from the store, so she left the bag of laundry for a minute with the Bersons. One time, a young woman was about to deliver a child, but couldn't make the climb up to the fourth floor. So she had the baby at the Bersons'.

Recently, Mr. Lachman complained "I went over to the Bersons', and how surprised I was to see total darkness in each window of their home. I was truly frightened. Who knew what had happened? Maybe they went to the country, or—God forbid—to visit a neighbor on another floor?" But this wasn't the case. After ringing without an answer, Mr. Berson finally came to the door.

"You'll forgive us," he started to explain. "We gave ourselves a *blekout* for a few minutes, and we wanted to hear the time on the radio."

"We were getting worried," Mr. Berson added. "It's already nine o'clock, and we haven't seen any of the regular guests!"

A Twenty Pound Turkey

I SEE THAT YOU'RE SOMEONE who also likes to reminisce about the old days.

Ah, the old days! Back then, who ever heard of such foolishness as a vacation? The rich went on vacation, or pleasure seekers, or those who have had enough 'consumption,' and by that I mean T.B.—may you be spared such misfortune.

But ordinary people knew that if work at the shop shut down because of the heat or slack, you'd run down to Canarsie or Coney Island.

You'd take the streetcar—it cost a nickel, and you'd travel maybe three hours for that price. A hot dog also cost a nickel, a glass of beer, a nickel, and a ride on the merry-go-round, another nickel.

So you could have a one-day vacation for fifteen or twenty cents.

Don't forget, we were younger then. Carefree, alone, nothing holding us back—if you wanted to take a girl out, it only cost another fifteen cents.

And believe me, I was a gentleman: I'd treat a girl to an ice cream soda—it only cost me a nickel!

But it's been forty or fifty years since those days, my friends. In that time people have improved their stations a little bit, and suddenly there's a wife, kids and grandkids to think about, and a new trend of going on vacation.

And who, you wonder, started this trend? The doctors! They want to relax for the summer so they advise their patients to follow them out to the country. And I was one of those suckers that followed doctor's orders!

You see, I went to the doctor for something minor, a small whistling cough. I knew that whistle from experience—years of smoking cigarettes—and that the cough was the whistle's accompaniment, like a piano to a violin.

The doctor checked me with his stethoscope and prodded me all over. Finally, he preached his sermon:

"First, you know that you're no longer a young man, and second, you must always remember that a man has two hands, two feet, two eyes, two nostrils, two rows of teeth, but only one heart. As they say—one heart per customer," he joked. "I recommend a vacation soon, and not a measly two-week trip, go away for six weeks."

So you see, I've been stuck here for six weeks. The strange thing is, the doctor told me to take a trip to the mountains, but warned me against venturing onto the slopes. Furthermore, he told me I had to lose twenty pounds, because, he told me, "You don't have the strength to be schlepping a twenty-pound turkey around all day, and taking him to bed each night. And if you don't listen to me, you and the turkey will soon be gone, leaving only the cranberries on the plate."

"What should I do?" I asked the doctor. This is what he told me: "You don't have to do anything. Just remember, at meals you have to either push the table away from yourself, or push yourself away from the table."

What would you have said to my doctor? Pushing a table, or pushing myself from the table—he calls this "doing nothing." And what does it mean to push the table away? I'd look crazy!

Imagine I'm sitting at a table with seven or nine other people, who have all paid their hard-earned money and want to eat. I'll tell you plain and simple, I don't think I have the heart to do it. I don't have the strength.

Nevertheless, he—the doctor—frightened away my appetite.

By breakfast I'm hungry again—I haven't eaten all night—but I have to count my calories. I'm no great mathematician, so I try to divide things up. I eat only a small piece of lox, a morsel of herring, a baked potato, a small roll with butter, a tiny bowl of cereal, two eggs, a cup of coffee, and a cookie smeared with jam.

Believe me, I have no trouble eating all of this. It's just that if I want to get up, to push myself from the table . . . It's like pushing a mountain.

And you wonder about lunch? Once again I see the twenty-pound turkey standing before me, gobbling: "Someone else will eat the cranberries!"

I grab a little bit of something to satisfy my appetite. After that a cup of soup, a piece of fish, three or four blintzes with sour cream, a little rice pudding with a cup of coffee, or milk, and nothing more! This is enough to make me sink into my chair. I can't move from the spot.

And I ask the hotel owner, why does your food sit so heavily? He jokes that he intentionally cooks stones so his guests will gain weight.

And for dinner? Better I don't talk about the banquet, because I barely made it out in one piece. Seriously, see for yourself.

They bring out a platter of chopped liver, that's appetizer number one, after that a plate with stuffed cabbage and a bit of tongue or something similar. That's appetizer number two. After this comes the soup, with a few matzoh balls swimming with noodles, farfle, or kasha.

Then a quarter chicken, or duck, or beef is served, plated on one side with carrot stew, and on the other side a little pudding or kishke. I'm telling you, even hearing about it makes your mouth water. On top of that, you eat all this with a slice of pickle or a bit of cabbage. It's so delicious, it calls out to you.

But what good is taste, when right after dinner I realize that even though I didn't have the chicken or duck, a new twenty-pound turkey is growing in my belly, and who knows who will want to eat the cranberries?

What? You laugh at me? You ask why I don't read a good book or a newspaper, or listen to music. Why eat all day and night? It's no easy task to sit and read with my tired eyes. And I tell you, if I didn't get up for a bicarbonate soda, I'd fall asleep at the table.

You laugh at the "soda-drinker!" You're just like the hotel owner. He says it's not all the eating that will break him, but all the soda we drink.

Imagine the nerve! It costs me 72 dollars a week to stay at the hotel, without tips, and now he thinks that I should bring my own bicarbonate.

I even asked him: "Mr. Kigler"—that's his name, our hotel owner—"How much bicarbonate do you think I drink? Three or four crates a week? Then charge me 80 cents and leave me in peace!"

The strange thing is, the hotel owner—out of spite it seems—served us turkey. The roast turkey stared me down and I stared back. I didn't eat it, as though we were sworn enemies . . .

But I won't be surprised if I get home and the doctor tells me there's still a twenty-pound turkey in my belly—and he's growing.

In the Hotel Kochalayn*

YOU LIKE TO TALK about baking in the sun. But when you're baking in the kitchen, you don't have the time to bake out in the sun. And when you're bathing in sweat, you won't have time to bathe out in the river.

By the time I turn off the stove and head out of the kitchen the big hand has turned and—the time is up.

Early in the morning, when the rooster crows and the well-to-do folks are finishing their card games from the night before—I am already on my feet. Here at the Hotel Kochalayn, it's like with certain diplomats at the UN: everyone wants to know what's cooking in their neighbor's pot . . . And finding a place at the stove is like getting a chair at the Eastern Wall. Whoever comes earliest can finish their prayers alone. And this is just for breakfast. Lunch is a different situation altogether.

Kochalayn (lit. "cook alone") hotels were destinations, notably in the Catskill Resort Region, that offered affordable accommodation with communal kitchens where guests cooked their own meals.

For the well off folks, there is half a day between breakfast and lunch. And I don't have to tell you what you could accomplish in half a day.

In half a day, you could lose the contents of your whole wallet playing cards, you could get sunburned laying outside until you look like a roasted duck. You could take a nap and have the sweetest dreams.

And if you want, you could read a book, a newspaper, and find out what's happening in the world. But who cares what you could do?

In the Hotel Kochalayn, before I buy my food for the day, an hour passes; once I get my few groceries put away in my small corner of the refrigerator, another hour has gone by. And do you think a potato just cooks itself? I have to peel it, wash it, chop it up, fill a pot with water, pour in the salt and—and then comes the important part: finding a place on the stove, where the pot can be assured a warm atmosphere. Because it often happens that the pot gets a cold reception, since one *kochalayn-nik* pushes the pot to one side, then another, to the other side. In the end, even if the pot is lucky enough not to fall to the ground, the potato soup is all congealed—as cold as jellied calves' feet.

This Cold War is fought every day.

And you think we don't have to keep an eye on the refrigerator? Recently I went to the fridge to get a bowl of strawberries I had set aside, and quickly realized that someone had made a "chop suey" of my berries. She had put a cup with cracklings and chicken fat on top of my bowl. The cup spilled and so when it came time to eat I had a bowl of strawberries with fried cracklings, topped with onion and chicken fat.

You say you like my cake? I like it too. But it didn't fall down from heaven. I tell you, that the cake wasn't just made from eggs, butter, and raisins. No, it's not that simple. It's also made with sweat and blood.

Antisemites slander the Jews, claiming that they bake blood into their matzoh, but that in Hotel Kochalayn people bake their cakes with blood—I can attest to personally...

The other day I woke up at dawn, slipped into the kitchen, and thought to myself: now, when everyone's asleep, I'll be able to cook a little and bake something. I grabbed the first ingredient to make a cake.

What? You want to know my recipe? How I made it? Don't you worry —I've got no shortage of recipes to share.

Grab a piece of paper and a pen and start writing: You take a little of the best flour, beat in the freshest eggs, put in a cup of the most refined sugar, throw in a box of the sweetest raisins, and mix in some salt according to your taste, add a pinch of cinnamon, a half ounce of whatever you'd like, and finally the correct measure of yeast. Mix it all together as well as you can, and let it sit until... until you put it in the oven. Then turn the oven up to the proper heat and let it bake for as long as it takes.

But one piece of advice—don't try the same trick that I tried the other day, when I got up at dawn to bake a cake.

What can I tell you? I made my cake—it literally shined. It rose so well that I stood over it, beaming with pride. I only wished that my grandchildren's fortunes would rise like my cake rose.

I put it in the oven, spit over my shoulder three times to ward off the Evil Eye—and then I lay down for a nap until the cake was ready to come out of the oven.

Well you can guess what happened. Out of nowhere, I heard a battalion marching into the kitchen. I generally don't like to squeeze myself into narrow spaces, but this time my heart told me to go into the kitchen to see what was cooking.

You should already know what happened—or do I need to spoon feed the answer to you?

What do you think? My cake burned? No, this time you guessed wrong.

A second woman had come in and felt a sudden urge to bake some fish. She had laid a few fish out on a tray—they looked like they were sunbathing. She didn't look, didn't think, just threw her tray of fish on top of my cake-pan.

My cake collapsed like a deflated balloon.

When the other women started to scold her, she quickly grabbed her tray of fish from the oven, and in her haste she slopped fish-broth onto my cake, and finished it off with some onions . . . In the end, my cake looked so bad, I wouldn't wish it on my worst enemies!!

Then the fish lady had the nerve to complain to me! "What the hell?" she exploded. "How can a woman lay around so casually, throwing a cake in the oven at God's mercy and catching a nap in the middle of the day, like an *alrightnik* on vacation!"

You wonder what happened in the end to the fish-cake monstrosity? That's a story for the history books.

One thing I'll tell you, that the *alrightniks* have never experienced such a misfortune. For a cake like this a rich woman would send her maid to guard the oven. And who knows? Maybe they would bring it to her table cooked to perfection. What? Don't you think she can afford it?

Brighton Beach

AM I HEARING YOU CORRECTLY? You're heading down to Brighton Beach for your vacation?

It's a strange thing—everyone swarms Brighton like moths swarming a lamp, even though there are plenty of vacation resorts: In the mountains, in California, in Arizona, Florida, Atlantic City, and many beaches and bays, oceans and rivers, hotels and motels. But they all decide on Brighton Beach.

"Then why are you here at Brighton Beach?" you may ask. It's probably the same story as yours. We thought of all the places we could go but we landed on Brighton—like a stone into water...

You see, I did the math with my wife: Going to the mountains would cost mountains of money. In a kochalayn—you spend the whole day boiling and baking—and then when you get home there's nothing to eat.

Traveling too far outside the city, my wife and children would spend the whole week feeling lonely, and when the weekend comes—and I finally come to meet them—there's sure to be a heavy rain, and though I spend the whole week dry . . . we'll be left high and dry out in the country.

And during all of this deliberating I heard about the beach from a friend. "In Brighton Beach, you'll feel right at home. You'll be free from the chaos of the city, from all the hu-ha, from having to squeeze yourself into trains and buses—you'll have a chance to rest your nerves."

And—as you can see—we are now in Brighton Beach, with Coney Island for a neighbor.

We've found a house—not anything I'd call a home. It's impossible to be on vacation and feel at home at the same time. As they say: you can't have your cake and eat it too.

To tell you the truth, it's not always so bad. There's a lot here that's actually quite nice. Occasionally it's quiet and restful, like a little patch of paradise on earth.

Have you ever gone out at two or three in the morning for a stroll on the boardwalk? I tell you, you can only find such silence in a cemetery. Everything is asleep. It seems to me that even the fish in the water are sleeping, and at times, it feels like the waves splash because it's cold and the fish are pulling at the covers.

What more do you need? You can find a seat—before the sun comes up there are plenty of places—and you can dream up the most beautiful things. You can pick out a perfect place in the sand and snooze like you would in the nicest hotel.

You see, our house in the Bronx is not so great. All day and all night you hear a racket outside. The elevated trains running by wake us up every fifteen minutes. The hum of the elevator in our building never stops.

And there are other annoyances, like the farewell of two lovebirds that seems to stretch on forever. It seems young people never look at the clock. As soon as one couple finishes their routine of laughing, singing, and making out, the elevator doors open and another couple is there to take their place. The sun finally comes up, and you haven't slept a wink.

The Brighton landlord tells us that here there is some mercy. Our neighbors in Coney Island aren't so lucky—they have it much worse. There the only people that sleep are the ones that buried themselves alive in the sand.

Of course, my vacation spot in Brighton Beach was not so easy to come upon.

I don't know how it is with your room, how large it is, or what you pay. But to find a place here, my wife and I sweated. We even went out on cold rainy days, because we had a plan: We told ourselves that when it is cold in Brighton Beach, the landlords go pecking around for whatever they can get, like hens on a cold day, especially in the poor section ... Because you should know that here in Brighton, there's an "Uptown" and a "Downtown," as they say around here: a rich Park Avenue, and an Orchard Street. The highest windows are untouchable, while in the lowest—where the poor folks can afford to stay—on a wet day you're basically wading through the muck.

Yes, I want to tell you how we went about finding rooms:

In one house, the people tried to entice us: "You'll breathe the same air as the rich. You don't have to throw a quarter into the meter down on the boardwalk to smell the exciting, salty air, like we once had to throw in a quarter for gas."

They assured us the rich haven't yet figured out how to put the sun in the freezer to cool off. We'd get the sun for free.

One woman really tried to sell us on the sand at the beach. Yes, she said, you should believe that the beach nearest to us is clean enough to eat off of. All day the waves sweep up and wash every grain of sand. "On top of that," she says, "you get the boardwalk for free. You can roll yourself out like dough all day and night, from Seagate to Manhattan Beach—you'll have the best time."

She had three rooms to rent but said that she had four, since she had two tenants who slept during the day, a man and wife who worked as servers all night. What's a poor *landlady* to do? The rents are so high you have to tie yourself in knots. So people: if there's room for two you can find a place for a third. And once you have three you can easily squeeze in a fourth.

You see, the room with kitchen privileges, like the one we have now, is right off the main street. But if you think it's all good, you'd be mistaken.

When we—me and my wife—came to look at the room, I asked the owner, "Tell me how much this chicken coop costs."

She laughed, and answered with another question: "How many chickens do you need to fit in it?"

"Me, my wife, and our two children," I said.

"Three hundred dollars for three months."

"And where," I asked, "is the closet for our things?"

"A closet?" she answered, "Whatever you brought your things in, that's where they should stay! What? You want to move in for good?"

"And what about the oven," my wife asked.

"In summer," joked the landlady, "an oven is not what you should be worrying about—it's not having a refrigerator that's the problem. I have the same problem. The landlord said to me, and I'll say the same thing to you, that if a fridge gets installed, you can use it."

Regardless, we will survive the summer, I just hope winter is not as harsh!

As my wife says, every day we spend here adds five years to our life. Look how old we are now, you can only imagine how long we've been renting at Brighton Beach.

The most important thing here, you understand, is the sun, the wonderful sun!

Dammit! I've been telling you to cover yourself up from the sun, but I forgot about it myself. I got so distracted talking to you, now I'm roasted like a turkey. At least my wife will have to stop calling me half-baked . . .

A Good Time

FOR THE MANY YEARS that Berl Landy worked in the shop, things were good during the working season, and meager during the slack season. Such things as vacations, country homes, relaxation, mountain getaways, summer resorts, winter resorts, camps, hot baths, salt baths—he only read about in the newspapers, or heard about from others at the market.

Someone told him about a holiday spot with a cool shining river to bathe in, with boats to sail, and beautiful places to fish. Hearing these stories, Berl would lose himself in fantasies and have to shake himself as if waking from a dream. He recalled how forty years ago, in the old country, he used to bathe in the river that flowed through his city. He swam faster than all the other children. And fish—he'd catch three-, or sometimes five-, even ten-pounders. And boats—he'd sail day and night on the water.

Now, Berl sighs, he bathes in sweat. Instead of catching fish, he tries to catch work where he can get it. And sailing? Ever since the ship that brought him to America, he hadn't seen a single boat, except for the picture on the calendar that hangs in the office of the shop.

Berl Landy was not just happy, but truly ecstatic, to send his wife and kids away to the country, if only to the infamous "*Hotel Kaptsn Kochalayn*." He beamed with joy when the family came back tanned and smiling.

Now his children were grown and married and they— Mr. and Mrs. Landy— didn't have the youthful vigor they once had. Both had acquired a touch of asthma, and a spot of rheumatism, and Berl especially had started to feel weak in his legs from forty years of pushing machine pedals in every shop he'd worked.

So Berl didn't argue with his wife when she suggested that this year they should go on vacation together. And not in a *kochalayn*, but a hotel with everything included.

Berl agreed and started to do the accounting—he'd take sixty dollars from the vacation fund in the union, a few dollars they'd put aside themselves, and together it all added up to a vacation. It would be a good time!

Mrs. Landy started buying everything—bit by bit—that she considered necessary for such a vacation, and Berl got busy making plans.

First he decided to search for a suitable destination. If they were going somewhere, he wanted a place with a river. Further, he wanted to test out his muscles and see how far he could swim, and maybe race boats, and go fishing.

He started looking in the papers for any advertised places, and called them on the phone. Here is a fine place, with too "fine" a price . . . the price of this one is on the right track, but the place is too far off-track—somewhere off in the middle of the woods.

When the Landys finally agreed on a place, Berl started to buy the things he needed. His wife explained: "You only live once, so when you buy something, buy the right thing. You wouldn't want to embarrass yourself."

The first thing Berl worried about was a suitcase. He understood that a suitcase was no small matter. He remembered the great role his suitcase played when he came to America. He reminded himself how he kept real Warsaw sausages and Polish biscuits in that suitcase, and how the cheap lock got jammed in the middle of the voyage and he went hungry until a locksmith could successfully break in.

Berl went from one store to the next, and at last bought himself a suitcase. The neighbors had to admit: with a suitcase like this, one could vacation as far away as Europe.

Another issue was buying a bathing suit. He had no idea how difficult it was for his wife when she bought one, and he was ashamed to admit that he looked through ten stores and in every place the sizes were either too small or too large. Not what he needed or wanted! But in the end, he had to take whatever he could find.

Berl also wanted to surprise his wife by dressing up elegantly when they got to the hotel, like he did in the old days when they first met. Back then, he wore a white linen suit, a straw hat, and yellow shoes. He started searching and threw a few things together.

He found it quite difficult to find the right equipment for fishing, but search long enough and you'll find what you're looking for.

When almost everything had been purchased and the date was quickly approaching, they had to arrange a proper vehicle to pick them up from their house and take them to the hotel.

And when everything was finally arranged, Berl sat down with his wife and began to calculate what it would cost them, and how much money they needed—for transportation, hotel, tips, and other expenses.

When his wife estimated her expenses, and Berl his, they realized that they were in dangerous territory, and it became clear: not only did they not have enough money for the hotel—they didn't even have enough money for the car to the hotel!

They looked at each other, then glanced at their suitcase with all their things.

Mrs. Landy blushed and said to herself, "there are thousands of people living all around us who never go on vacation who get their tans sitting up on their roofs.

Thousands travel to places near the city—to a park, to Coney Island. We've lived long enough without the country—and we'll keep living!"

Berl could not so easily make peace with the idea of giving up a trip to the country. He muttered to himself, "It serves me right! One should count more with the head than with the feet. Walk before you run . . ."

However, he did not want to upset his wife, so he laughed, "Next year, if we're still alive, we'll be able to try out our new clothes but for now, let's make something to eat and head to Coney Island—It will be a good time!

The Battle Over a Ball

WHEN MY LITTLE ones used to come in off the street or home from school, their voices hoarse from yelling about some game of throwing balls around, I didn't have the slightest idea what this game was about, what it was called, who the players were that young and old alike were going crazy over, ready to jump at you if you said even one nice thing about the other team.

But I caught on slowly and learned from my chanting and panting children that the game was called *beysbol*, and the two battling armies were the *yenkis* and the *dadzhers*.

It took me a while to come around to the idea that this was a game, and not some rare disease, since I was always hearing about "*dadzher-yenki*" and "*yenki-dadzher*" until it started to sound to my ears like "*yenk-itis*" and "*dadzher-itis*"—like "*tonsilitis*" and "*arthritis*"—may you never know such misfortune. To tell the truth, there were times at the beginning when I heard the kids yelling "*yenkis*" and "*dadzhers*" and I wanted to run for the doctor!

However, as they grew older I grew a little smarter, I started to understand why they were always at each other's throats. In the middle of the night they chased each other. As I lay dreaming I heard them call out the worst names. Over time I began to put together who were the hasidim and who were the rebbes of the sport. I also started to understand that in this game, instead of the rebbe blessing the hasidim, the hasidim bless the rebbe. And the "prayers" are demands that they use their hands, use their feet, and sometimes—their heads.

So you see that as you live to be older, you get a little smarter...

When the children would bring home pictures of their heroes, I learned that some were good runners, some were good hitters, that there's a *pitcher*, and that someone can hit a *hom-ron*—meaning no one can get him.

Of course, one group of hasidim brought pictures of the *yenkis* and the others, the *dadzhers*, and all of them wanted me to follow their rebbe.

You wouldn't envy what went on in my home. When the *yenkis* and the *dadzhers* play each other, they have free time afterwards to rest, make plans, and to share a meal. But at my place an inferno burns day and night... in my house balls, bats, and beatings fly without end.

My daughter came home and hung a picture of her favorite *dadzher*, which showed him slamming a ball to beat the *yenkis*. Then came my son who brought a picture of his hero, from the *yenkis*, and demonstrated with a bat how the miracle player hit a *homer* . . . he gave a hard swing and it broke my glasses! But he hung his picture up right over his sister's picture of the *dadzhers*.

If only you could see my daughter when she came back into the house. The house became a field, the children split up into teams and—it was a nasty game. Both started running around the table like they'd hit a *hom-ron*. By the second ining they were bouncing off the walls.

What more can I tell you. Both of their heroes came falling down—they were torn from the wall. And with them went flying lamps, glassware, and what would be a baseball game without pitchers. Only now mine are broken, frames and all . . .

All night the pictures went flying up and down, until their mother—thank God!—called out to them "Children! Even a world war must eventually come to an end. You—bring the *yenkis* to your bed. You—bring the *dadzhers* to your bed, and let there be peace in this house again!"

They obeyed their mother's wishes—but both teams slept with bats in their bed . . .

Now, since the children came to understand they needed to have more education than physical education, they have a new perspective on the game and on their heroes.

Recently my son said to me, "Dad, I have a ticket to a baseball game, and since I can't make it would you like to go? By now you are a real expert," I lit up at his suggestion.

It was true, the children had shown me how to go, how to see, how to hear, and they even told me how I should yell when one of their heroes did something great.

And now, my friends, since you already know about the diseases of *yenki-itis* and *dadzher-itis*, I will tell you more...

I went to a place that looked like a fairground, and what I noticed the most was the yelling. Everyone was yelling! They yelled the whole time, even when no one was on the field, and as I understand, the yelling is like the prayer "*who will live and who will die*"—who should come in and who should be thrown out...

When the game started, I found that to my right was a *yenki-hasid*, and to my left was a *dadzher-fen*. Of course, I remained completely neutral. I am not versed enough in the game to give you a play-by-play account, but the reactions on every side of me let me know what was going on.

When something from the right side knocked into me, jostling my hat, I knew that the *yenkis* were on the field. When something from the left side poked me in the back, ringing in my left ear, and pulling my shirt, I knew that the *dadzhers* had seized the diamond...

What can I tell you, in the first inning, when someone got a hit, I felt that I'd gotten hit myself... But when the next time around, there was a *straykaut*, it seemed like I had lost the score and lost the hat on my head.

Who won? This is all I can say: my son might have paid five dollars for the ticket, but I—I paid with a new hat, a new shirt, a bruise on my side, two teeth, and the hair on my head . . . You really want me to tell you the outcome of the game, when you didn't suffer, and you have all the teeth in your mouth? One thing I will tell you: I was right to say that this lively game is something of an illness, otherwise you wouldn't pay me a visit, like a patient, to find out how I felt after the game.

But to tell the truth—we'd all be better off if we knew that wars, like baseball games, would eventually come to an end.

Cooling System

THE FREIDINS live in three small rooms on the third floor of their building. And just as the frost likes to visit their home during the winter months, the sun loves to vacation in the Freidin's home over the summer. And until it gets dark, it refuses to leave the house. It seemed to take great pleasure from burning—and from roasting others...

Since the summer, with its heat, became an all too frequent guest, the practical Mrs. Freidin looked for some kind of solution. Mostly, she was looking out for her three children. She dreamed often of traveling to the country, but this was merely a dream—she knew their financial situation. And even if they managed to get away for a couple weeks, as soon as they came back the sun would be there to greet them, blazing across the carpet, even hotter than when they left—and the question of the heat would not be solved.

Mrs. Freidin was a practical woman. She had come to an agreement with her husband and children when it came to buying a television. She convinced them that a television was only good in someone else's home: if they want to watch something on TV, they could go to the neighbors', if they don't, they shouldn't go. But if they had a television in their own home, day and night every child and their parents would be over to watch. And if they wanted to go out, it wouldn't be appropriate to leave the guests alone in the house, so they'd spend all of their time cautiously taking care of their visitors, making sure they were fed if they got hungry.

But, Mrs. Freidin argued with her husband, a *cooling system* is something different entirely. It would be worthwhile even if they had to get it on credit.

She started to count the reasons down on her fingers: "We won't have to flee to the country," that's one finger. "We won't have to hide out at the movies," that's a second finger. "We won't have to travel somewhere to swim," a third. "We don't need to run to the candy store to cool off" is a fourth finger. The remaining finger indicated that they should, indeed, buy a *cooling system* for their home right away.

"Now imagine the joy," becoming more inspired by her brilliant plan, "when everyone else is melting in the heat, we'll be sitting in the house and it will be nice and cold—such a pleasure—even if we have to put on sweaters."

So Mrs. Freidin convinced her husband that they should buy a cooling machine.

Imagine how happy the children were when, on a hot day, two workers came to the house, with the necessary tools. They brought up a large box and unpacked "Winter" on a summer day. They promptly got to work, installing the cooling-system in the children's room.

They sweated a few hours to block every hole in the window, closed the door, and with one turn of a dial the machine started blustering like an *alrightnik* at the Eastern Wall.

The children ran to tell their friends in the neighborhood that they could play inside all day.

The neighbor children brought their friends from across the street and the children told their mothers to bring lunch because they'd be over at the Freidins'. Of course, the mothers also made themselves something to nibble on while enjoying the cold atmosphere.

It wasn't long before all the neighbors found out about the "Winter" at the Freidins' house. The first couple of days, people came out of curiosity, to see how the machine worked and how it could cool down the heat. Then they started coming by to cool off.

One neighbor showed up, carrying her child in one hand and a plate of food in the other, and said, "You've done a *mitzvah* saving my child. In your place we can eat. I felt like at any moment I would burst into flames at my place—and I didn't want to wait to find out."

A second mother sent over her young daughter in the morning to play, and in the evening would come over with her older girl, who was attending summer school, so she could do her homework.

"When my daughter comes to your place, she forgets that it's summer school and doesn't sweat about her learning."

Among the neighbors came one who asked for a small favor: her daughter—pregnant with her first child—needed a place to give birth. The woman asked if the Freidins would lend her a bed in the bedroom—where the air conditioner was—for one week until the baby came.

A man who suffered from asthma, would, on particularly hot nights, drop by for a while, claiming his cough felt much better with a cooling-machine.

Well, I won't bore you with the details: the whole evening Mrs. Freidin had to make hot tea and hot coffee. Others wanted warm milk, anything to warm themselves up from the *cooling system* that was taking over the house...

The upshot of this was that everyone dragged chairs in from the front room into the bedroom to have a good seat, and the Freidins themselves had to stand in the kitchen and prepare snacks.

Meanwhile, the issue still on the Freidins mind was: where will the children sleep?

The guests sat in the room with the cooler until one or two o'clock, when the children stretched out to go to sleep, to lay down their tired heads . . .

But if you think that Mrs. Freidin is the only practical one you'd be forgetting about her husband. He finally found the best way to get the guests out of the house right at ten o'clock. That's when the fuse just happened to burst and the electricity went out. "Now," Mr. Freidin said, "we'll be happy and feel refreshed. It might be hot, but what a relief that the neighbors have scattered away!"

A Televi . . . shhh!

YOU DON'T HAVE A TELEVISION YET? If so then I'm in luck—You can still hold a conversation! Let's talk a minute.

I tell you, since the TV came around, friends are no longer friends, neighbors are no longer neighbors, and in the house you only hear one word: "Shh!"

In my house, we hear nothing more than "shhh." A little about me: I have a wife, and kids, and the kids gave us grandchildren. You should come by some time to see my place.

My television gets nine channels, and on every channel is a different show. The women want to watch one thing, the men a second thing, and the grandchildren—they have their own favorites.

I'm sure I don't have to tell you what takes place every evening in my house. On TV there's wrestling, prize fights, dance, singing, and comedy—with plenty of *komoyshels*. But in our home, there are only prize fights. To tell the truth, there isn't even really a prize. But the fights—I don't wish them for myself and I don't wish them for you.

My daughter loves to watch dance, my son loves to watch wrestling, my mother loves to watch the comedians, and the grandchildren love to watch kids' shows.

Someone turns the TV to one channel, another one gets up and changes it. A third comes to put on something else. What can I tell you? Fists fly, and there isn't even a referee to put an end to it, like in a prize fight, where at least the bell would stop the action.

Recently they really went at it, until the television screen cracked! And what do you think the result was? It cost me eight dollars to replace the screen!

I'll tell you what I wish for the inventor of the television. Not to sit in prison, not to work a day for my boss in the shop, not to suffocate in the subway at rush-hour when people are standing on his toes. No, I only wish that he should spend an evening at my house and hear all the racket and screaming—"Shhh!!" and *he* would get hit with the slaps that fly from one person to the other.

Once I wanted to go out to a Worker's Society meeting, to hear what was new and to chat a little bit. But even there I couldn't escape . . . One person's favorite show didn't end until 9:00, so he got to the meeting at 9:30. Someone else's show ended at 9:30, so he got there at 10. Others showed up at 10:30 and 11. It's impossible to have a meeting these days since everyone has to wake up at six in the morning to get to work or start looking for work.

I say, the Society should just buy nine TVs, split up into nine different rooms, and announce: "Come in time to watch TV," then, you'll see, the members will show up on time for the meeting.

What more do you want? I recently went to a wedding where the father of the bride was an hour late to the party. Everyone was running around like chickens with their heads chopped off. And what had happened? Nothing terrible: the bride's father wanted to finish watching a *quiz-show*. Only then did he turn off the TV and join the dance.

Since we're on the subject, I'll tell you a story that my Society brother shared with me.

He, the Society brother, went to visit a sick member. He dragged himself up four flights of stairs, caught his breath and knocked on the door.

Someone opened the door and invited him into a dark room where a television was roaring loudly. They slipped him a chair but instead of a welcoming "*hello*," he received a collective "SHH!!" from all of the visitors.

"Shh!" is "Shh!" in the end! So he sat down to look at the "box" for an hour and a half until finally the game ended. The house lit up again and as he started to ask how our sick friend was doing, someone answered that the sick man lived next door, and no one had any idea how he was doing . . . In the end, instead of being greeted by the sick man, he was met with a headache from sitting in a dark, packed room without a breath of fresh air.

A *landsman* told me another story: he longed to speak with his children and grandchildren, who lived two thousand miles away. He called up and his grandson Isaac David answered the phone. My *landsman* didn't even have the opportunity to ask if everyone was healthy before his grandson shouted "*Zeyde*! Get it over with!"

The *zeyde* answered: "Isaac David, don't worry about it, I have enough quarters with me—so I can speak with all of you."

But the grandson just as quickly yelled back into the telephone, "*Zeyde*, we're right in the middle of a TV show, call back later!"—and hung up the phone without so much as a "Goodbye."

What? You have a story to tell me about your luck with the television? You'll have to excuse me and tell me another time, because my favorite show is starting pretty soon—I wouldn't give it up for anything. If you want to watch, you can come over to my place . . . But remember: "Shh!!"

GLOSSARY

Boytshik [בויטשיק]
American Yiddish. Boy or young man, usually as a term of endearment.

Chometz [חמץ/*khomets*]
Leavened bread, or any other fermented food, which are forbidden during Passover and must be removed from the home.

Hasid, Hasidim [חדר/*khosed, khsidim*]
Follower of a branch of orthodox Judaism originating in the 18th century which rapidly gained popularity throughout Eastern Europe. The central characteristics of Hasidism include allegiance to a particular Rebbe, or spiritual leader, emphasis on individual prayer, and joyous worship involving singing, and dancing.

Kaptsn [קבצן]
Pauper.

Kheyder [חדר/*kheyder*]
Also spelled Cheder/Heder. Traditional Jewish religious school for boys from around age five up to Bar Mitzvah. Study centers on learning Hebrew and the first five books of the Torah.

Khupe (חופה)
Wedding canopy.

Landsman (לאַנדסמאַן)
Compatriot; person from the same town or region.

Mezuzah (מזוזה/*mezuze*)
Small parchment sroll inscribed with certain verses of the Torah, attached by observant Jews to their doorposts inside a small tube made of metal or wood.

Mistsvah (מיצווה/*mitsve*)
Good deed or commandment. While Gentiles are expected to follow the Ten Commandments, the Torah contains 613 commandments which an observant Jew must endeavor to follow.

Nudnik (נודניק)
A bore or nuisance.

Rebbe (רבי/*rebe*)
Here: a teacher in a kheyder. More broadly a rebbe can be a spiritual leader/mentor or Hasidic rabbi.

Shabbos (שבת/*shabes*)
Also spelled Shabbes/Shabbat. The Jewish Sabbath. Beginning at sundown on

Friday evening and ending on Saturday evening at dusk. Traditionally observant Jews are forbidden from all forms of work on Shabes, including handling money, writing, travelling or making fire.

Shikse [שיקסע/*shikse*]
Also spelled shiksa. Non-Jewish girl or woman (Pejorative).

Zeyde [זיידע]
Grandfather.

Translator's Postface

While working at the Yiddish Book Center in Amherst, MA, I stumbled upon a small book of songs *"Zingen Mir Far Sholem,"* published in 1965. I began excitedly flipping through this compilation, surely a product of a group of young anti-war Yiddishists. However, I was astounded and confounded to find, instead, a portrait of a smiling man in his seventies, with large glasses and a bowtie: Sam Liptzin. This launched my journey to learn about this man and to discover the depths of his work.

Sam Liptzin, known variously throughout his career as *Kvekzilber* (Quicksilver), and *Feter Shepsl*, and *Onkl Sam*, was born March 13, 1893 in Lipsk, Belarus. He emigrated to the United States in 1909, where his uncle found him a job in a men's clothing shop. He became active in socialist politics during his teenage years, first contributing to the movement by selling socialist literature on the streets of New York, and publicly announcing meetings and events. During one of these announcements, Liptzin made a joke that prompted an invitation from the night's speaker to introduce the program, launching his career as a public persona. Liptzin recalls seeing his joke printed in the *Forverts* the following day, with a caption reading "hear what the griner yingl–the Greenhorn–said last night."

He soon began writing professionally, contributing jokes to various publications, including *Der Groyser Kundes*, and *Di Varheyt*, later publishing his own, short lived, monthly humor magazine, *Der Humorist*. Most notably, Liptzin contributed to the Communist-affiliated *Morgn Frayhayt*, where he wrote a regular column—"*A vort far a vort*" ("A Word for a Word") —for several decades. Over the next sixty years, Liptzin published regular collections of short stories, poems, one-act plays, aphorisms, and songs totaling thirty volumes—including two in English translation—by the time he died on September 22, 1980.

Throughout his life Sam Liptzin remained a dedicated *kempfer*—fighter—in labor and union demonstrations and disputes. As such, he had several run-ins with organized crime, including a beating and attempted kidnapping that prompted a lengthy recovery period in Florida. Liptzin lived most of his life in New York, in neighborhoods including the Lower East of Manhattan, Coney Island, and the Allerton Coops—the colloquial designation of the United Worker's Cooperative Colony, a complex built in the Bronx in the 1920s, populated predominantly by Communist Party affiliated Jewish garment workers. Liptzin's active participation within the movement and residential proximity to leftist workers framed the ideological force of his writing, which was concerned with the everyday lives of leftist Yiddish speakers, featuring humorous situations based around familiar characters, environments, and circumstances.

The title of the first translated collection of Sam Liptzin's work, *In Spite of Tears*, serves as a guiding ethos of the author's entire body of work. In the foreword to the collection, Liptzin explains his unique combination of humor and serious, political subject matter: "*In spite of tears*, however, it must be clear to all that we must persist in the struggle for a better life, of joy and good fortune for all humanity." He expresses a desire for the reader to "give his earnest reflection to the problems of men and women who are still seriously oppressed and enslaved today," while hoping that "my pen can call forth a smile among the many who ply their daily toil, weighed down by their poverty and insecurity of life." This foreword reveals Liptzin's approach: a humorous portrayal of serious issues written *about* the worker and *for* the worker. *In Spite of Tears* also highlights the centrality of the American context in Liptzin's work. Almost all of the stories take place in the United States, with a majority of them set in New York City.

"I Am an American!," a cornerstone of *In Spite of Tears* is a passionate testimony rejecting anti-immigrant sentiment. In the introductory paragraph, Liptzin implores those that "rant... against everything progressive" to "turn your finger around, and point it at yourself—there is the enemy, the foe of all mankind." He claims his patriotism, detailing his love for the beauty of America. He explains, "my citizenship is the work of thirty years," enumerating the labor provided by immigrants who build and sustain the industry and success of the United States, from the sweatshops of New York, to the coal mines of Scranton, to the steel mills of Pittsburgh, to the auto plants of Detroit. He recognizes the "alien" parents of Eddie Cantor, Irving Berlin, and George Gershwin, whose art came to define American culture. He cites, as well, Albert Einstein and Lise Meitner, "aliens" who theorized atomic power, and thus shaped 20th century society.

Liptzin's books often featured testimonials that, while certainly self-selected for praise, offer insight into how Sam Liptzin was regarded by his peers: important figures in the leftist press and literature. Moyshe Olgin notes that "Sam Liptzin is one of the most loved folk storytellers and entertainers on the proletarian front," claiming that "Sam Liptzin has put forward his own genre through his writings." Another *Frayhayt* editor, Paul Novick, calls Liptzin a "true *folks-shrayber*,—folk writer" praising him that he has "not lost contact with the times." Samuel Sillen, a writer for the English language *Daily Worker,* claims "Liptzin is a folk writer. He deals with everyday themes in a warm, human way. Here are plain people seen with all their failings and their virtues." Moishe Katz comments that "Liptzin has a keen eye and can recognize true comic situations in very common circumstances, where another would not think of looking at all." Taken together, these reviews demonstrate that Liptzin was largely successful in his goal of producing humorous literature that both reached and reflected the working masses, of which he considered himself an active and passionate part. In the foreword to his 1955 collection of poems *A vort far a vort*, he emphasizes that he does not want to be removed from the everyday life of the workers, explaining that "I need to find time to share with my sisters and brothers in their struggle."

These descriptions highlight Sam Liptzin as an important writer of the mid-twentieth century, someone who consistently had his finger on the pulse of radical politics in America. Yet, he is seldom mentioned in histories of Yiddish-American literature. This volume is an attempt to remedy that. Taken predominantly from his post-WWII work, these selections highlight Liptzin's wit and charm as he not only confronts the political condition of mid-twentieth century America, but also meditates on growing older.

I hope that a younger, twenty-first century audience will find Sam Liptzin a worthy peer. Years before social media revolutionized content creation and intricate communication networks, Liptzin developed a supportive community of readers that funded his work throughout his career and spread his influence across the nation. The Sam Liptzin Book Committee, whose name features prominently on the title pages of many of Liptzin's later volumes, was composed predominantly of Yiddish speakers who, like Liptzin himself, were workers in the needle trade and invested Leftists. Through the support of this committee, which had a presence in cities across America, Liptzin was able to publish for decades as well as travel prolifically, through book tours which brought him into contact with fans and comrades from Atlantic to Pacific.

Sam Liptzin presents us with a spirit which continues to be relevant. As the struggle continues against the ravages of capitalism: the parasitic landlords and greedy bosses, we might turn, for guidance, to Liptzin, who wrote poignantly and bitingly about these very same topics a century ago. While Sam Liptzin's portrait on the back of *Zingen Mir Far Sholem* was the face of a man with many decades of wisdom under his belt, the youthful spirit I expected from the volume shines through decades of Liptzin's work. I hope that this collection of translations introduces a new generation to the work of Sam Liptzin, and that they may find inspiration and laughter within these pages.

Sam Liptzin

Sam Liptzin—also known as Feter Shepsl, Uncle Sam, and Kvikzilber (Quicksilver)—was a self-proclaimed "radical humorist." Born in Lipsk, Belarus, in 1893, Liptzin moved to the United States in 1909 and became active in leftist politics as an organizer, speaker, and writer. For much of his career, he wrote a regular column in the Morgen Freiheit—the Yiddish Communist journal. Writing through the 1970s, Liptzin published twenty-eight volumes of short stories, poems, and aphorisms.

Liptzin in English Translation

In Spite of Tears : Short Stories, Humoresques, Sketches, monologues, Aphorisms, Trans. S.P. Rudens, Amcho, 1946.

Zeke Levine is a New York City based musician, musicologist, and translator. His work focuses on American culture of the twentieth century, with particular attention to the development of Yiddish-American music. As a scholar, Levine has presented research in venues across the United States and in Europe. As a translator, Levine's work has been featured in the Yiddish Book Center's *Pakn Treger*, and *In Geveb*. As a 2019-2020 Yiddish Book Center Translation Fellow, Levine translated a wide body of Sam Liptzin's works, a selection of which is featured in this volume.

FARLAG

Farlag Press is an independent publisher run by a collective of translators and literature-lovers. We prioritise translations from stateless and minority languages, as well as the writings of exiles, immigrants and other outsiders.

We are a strictly for-loss company, though we are registered as a non-profit association in France.

www.farlag.com

Also Available

1. Moyshe Nadir *Messiah in America (A Drama in Five Acts)*
Translated by Michael Shapiro
144pp ISBN: 9791096677047

2. Miriam Karpilove *Judith: A Tale of Love & Woe*
Translated by Jessica Kirzane
146pp ISBN: 9791096677108

3. Zusman Segalovitsh *Tsilke the Wild*
Translated by Daniel Kennedy
292pp ISBN: 9791096677115

4. Anna Margolin *During Sleepless Nights and Other Stories*
Translated by Daniel Kennedy
88pp ISBN: 9791096677122

Farlag Bilingual Series:

1. Hersh Dovid Nomberg *À qui la faute ?* ‎װער איז שולדיק
(Édition bilingue: yiddish/français)
Traduit par Fleur Kuhn-Kennedy
66pp ISBN: 9791096677085

2. Hersh Dovid Nomberg *Between Parents* ‎צווישן טאַטע־מאַמע
(Bilingual edition: Yiddish/English)
Translated by Ollie Elkus and Daniel Kennedy
74pp ISBN: 9791096677092

www.ingramcontent.com/pod-product-compliance
Lightning Source LLC
LaVergne TN
LVHW061038070526
838201LV00073B/5087